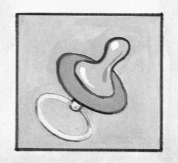

To my grandmother,
Ida Morrow Miesner

RACHEL M ROBERTS

Babies, Babies, Babies

Written and illustrated
by Kathy Wilburn

A GOLDEN BOOK • NEW YORK
Western Publishing Company, Inc., Racine, Wisconsin 53404

The bright sun comes up
And brings a new day,
The world sings to baby,
"Please come out and play!"

Baby is hungry
For good things to eat,
Sweet berries and cream
Make breakfast a treat.

Babies love sunshine,
And rides in the park,
Puppies for hugging,
And playing till dark.

Baby and kitty
Play hide-and-go-seek;
Close your eyes tight,
And try not to peek.

All babies will cry
Because they are sleepy,
Wet, hungry, or scared
By something that's creepy!

They wonder at stars
That dance in the sky,
At rainbows that glow,
And the moon way up high.

Crawling and climbing,
How fast baby goes!
Upstairs and downstairs,
On knees and on toes.

So many new things
To learn day by day,
Fingers, toes, numbers,
And fun games to play.

Guess who is ready
For sun by the sea;
On warm summer beaches,
Baby laughs and runs free.

Now see what baby
Has in each hand,
A pail and a shovel
To make castles of sand.

Snowflakes are falling
On baby's cheeks and nose,
Mittens keep hands warm
When winter wind blows.

Babies love tumbling
Beneath winter's sun,
Making snow angels
Is always such fun!

Inside the toy chest
Are a pull-car and blocks,
Beanbag and Teddy,
And a pony that rocks.

With sisters and brothers
Babies love sharing
Bright, happy hours,
Playing and caring.

Bathtime is merry,
With bubbles that wiggle,
And slippery soap
That makes baby giggle.

Babies love stories
Of faraway places,
Where brightly striped tigers
Have great jungle chases.

Mommy and Daddy
Tuck baby in bed,
They both softly say,
"Good night, sleepyhead."

Nights are for dreaming
Of fairies with wings,
And magical lands
Where the nightingale sings.

Babies, babies, babies,
Dream sweet dreams tonight,
And smile gentle smiles
Till the day's new light.